White Rabbit's Colour Book

Alan Baker

KING*f*ISHER

KINGFISHER
An imprint of Kingfisher Publications Plc
New Penderel House, 283-288 High Holborn
London WC1V 7HZ

First published in paperback by Kingfisher 1995
This edition published in 1998
4 6 8 10 9 7 5 3
3 (3TR)/0199/TWP/PW/NYM 170
Originally published in hardback by Kingfisher 1994

Copyright © Alan Baker 1994

A CIP catalogue record for this book
is available from the British Library

ISBN 1 85697 399 9

Printed in Singapore

One day White Rabbit found
three big pots of paint,
red, yellow and blue.

Sunshine yellow,
she thought.
Lovely.

A quick dip
and ...

... yellow rabbit,
bright as the sun.

Now what about red,
thought Rabbit.

What's this?
Orange Rabbit?
Look. Red and yellow
together make
orange!

Time for
a wash,
thought
Rabbit.

Red on its own this time.

Splash!

Red Rabbit,
sizzling hot red.

How cool blue looks, thought Rabbit.

What's this? Purple Rabbit?
Look. Red and blue
together make purple.
I'm a very important
Royal Purple
Rabbit.

Princess
Purple
Rabbit
in the shower.

Blue will do,
thought Rabbit.

Blue Rabbit,
icy cold blue.
Brrr.

How warm
yellow looks,
thought Rabbit.

What's this?
Green Rabbit.
Look. Blue
and yellow
together make
green!

Oh dear,
no more
water.

All that's left is
a little red paint.

Now what would happen? thought Rabbit.

Hooray! Brown Rabbit. Lovely warm brown.
Blue, yellow, and red together make brown.
And brown's just right for me.